OTHER BOOKS by ROZ CHAST

LAST RESORTS
UNSCIENTIFIC AMERICANS
PARALLEL UNIVERSES
POEMS AND SONGS

MONDO BOXO

CARTOON STORIES BY ROZ CHAST

1817

HARPER & ROW, PUBLISHERS, New York

Cambridge, Philadelphia, San Francisco, Washington

London, Mexico City, São Paolo, Singapore, Sydney

For Bill and Ian

Designer: C. Linda Dingler

Library of Congress Catalog Card Number: 87-45029
ISBN: 0-06-015795-X
Manufactured in Italy by Arti Grafiche Amilcare Pizzi, S.p.A.

87 88 89 90 91 10 9 8 7 6 5 4 3 2 1

FIRST U.F.O.

We were all sitting around the kitchen table at Ann's.

The topic under discussion was fish.

Neon tetras? I like 'em.

You ought to get an aquarium.

Tim was feeling rather silent, so he said nothing.

There was a little tension in the air, but it was tolerable.

It was around 9:35 when someone noticed the light out the kitchen window.

Hey! What's that?

I remember, because I could half-hear the theme of "The Patsy Parker Show" coming from the living-room.

IT'S THE PATSY PARKER SHOW

It was definitely not the moon.

We all got excited because it looked so much like a UFO.

FACT or FANCY?
UFO magazine
UFOLOGIST QUARTERLY
UFO'S: NO BIG JOKE!
FLYING SAUCERS
THE UFO GUIDE

We went out to investigate.

Some people were skeptical.

It's a weather balloon.

Others gave it the benefit of the doubt.

I just know it's _something_.

R. Chast

The Museum of Norman L.

First, let's meet the caretakers, Mr. and Mrs. L.

Here is the very spoon with which Norman L. took his first bite of solid food.

SPOON

You might want to peruse the toys which Norman first played with as a tot.

FUFFY

PLEASE DO NOT LEAN ON GLASS!

You are now in one of the most sacred shrines of all: The Room of the Blanket.

"BABA"
No photographs, please.

Mr. and Mrs. L. would be all too pleased to show you some of the garments of the young lad.

Perhaps you are wondering, what about the mind? What was the mind of Norman all about?

JULY 1963

Well, why don't you spend a couple of days in the Normanic Archives and find out?

REPORT CARDS
1959 - 1975

MATH EXAMS
1961 - 1975

ENGLISH EXAMS

NORMAN'S POETRY
1957 - 1979

BOOK REPORTS
1961 - 1965

BOOK REPORTS

Remember, every Tuesday is Movie Night.

But come anytime— the Museum is always open.

THE MUSEUM OF NORMAN
4-N

WELCOME

R. Chast

THE PERFECT FAMILY

They don't use very much salt—

—but when they do, it's SEA salt.

And not just from any old sea; it's from a particular part of a particular sea.

SLÖNOTZVITA SEA

Please take a good look at the label, because if you try to buy some, you will probably get the wrong brand.

SEA SALT

Here they are, chuckling at you in advance.

HA HEE NG
HA HA
HOO HA
HEE
HEE

There's much, much more, but it's really too horrible to go into.

WORKING OUT WITH THE PERFECTS

THOSE BUSY, BUSY PERFECTS

WHY WE'RE GLAD LITTLE JUDY IS TOTALLY TRI-LINGUAL

THE PERFECTS AND ALL THEIR FRIENDS

THE PERFECTS RENOVATE DEN FOR ONLY $150,000.00

MRS. PERFECT MAKES CENTERPIECE OUT OF OLD CAULIFLOWER

R. Chast

POETS ON STRIKE

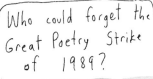

Who could forget the Great Poetry Strike of 1989?

It began as a small "work slowage" in Cranston, R.I. ~

"Forget it - I'm not rushin' for nobody."

~and escalated into the biggest, longest-lasting strike this particular art had ever known.

"La, la, la"

Word spread. Poets' demands were made known to their bosses and also to the public.

OUR DEMANDS:
① Higher wages.
② Better working conditions.
③ 2 weeks' paid vacations per year.

People were thrown into a dither, fearful of poetry shortages.

"What are we going to DO???"

Some were supportive; others were not.

"Those poor dears!"

"So they think the world owes 'em a living, huh?"

Non-poet scabs were bused in from coast to coast.

"What do you want me to write?"

Their work was so inferior that industry captains were forced to meet the demands of the strikers.

"Roses are red, Violets are blue, Sugar is white..."

Finally, after 6½ months, an agreement was reached, and even the most depressed poet was happy, sort of.

R. Chast

Bob's Thoughts Fly Away

Mendelssohn's Concerto of the Exhausted in D-Minor, played by the Hackensack Symphony Orchestra...

La, la, la...

La, la... little duck falling off a ladder?

No, no... only the violinist... soup... WHO SAID SOUP? Cream of wheat...

What's that word spell? Oh... it's the curtain...

... Alexander, that's Nancy's son... the one with the Junior Mints...

... ha, ha, Ethel Merman's shoe... WAKE UP, BOB!!!

Lamb chops dressed in little skirts - Cellists... uh oh...

r. Chast

Picnic of Long Ago

The days get longer and longer, 'til finally it's summer.

Sweaters are discarded, even at night.

Winter coats have never even existed.

The sun sets slowly and the sky stays turquoise blue for a long time.

Far away, one can hear the sound of a Bungalow Bar truck.

BUNGALOW BAR, IT TASTES LIKE TAR, THE MORE YOU EAT IT, THE SICKER YOU ARE.

The last days of school are the hardest. Who can take anything seriously?

June eventually turns into July and we go to "the country", or "upstate."

Sam and I pack our toys in big shopping bags.

The rest is packed for us, sometime when we're out playing, because we never see it done.

Everything gets loaded into the car.

In about 5 hours, we are there, slightly sick on too many grapes and cheese and crackers.

A couple of days go by. We settle in.

On our third night, a neighbor invites us to a picnic for the following evening. We can hardly wait.

In a grove, someone has strung Chinese lanterns. We are carrying rice pudding, our family's contribution. It is a warm, breezy night.

There is a smell of hot dogs and hamburgers in the air. People are grilling away.

There are about 100 adults and 20 or so kids. We play tag, run around, fall.

Sam remembers a line of 3 or 4 picnic tables pushed together and covered with bowls of potato salad, cole slaw, relish, macaroni salad, etc., but I don't.

I remember a lady in a red and white checked dress handing me a tumbler of soda in front of a starry sky.

R. Chast

The Adventures of Fifi, Urban Canine

Fifi wasn't but two years old when she told her owner that she wanted more independence.

She thought it was about time she got to go out on her own in the afternoons.

She wanted to walk up and down the avenue, stopping in one pet boutique or another—

or perhaps having her fur done if she was in the mood.

Many other dogs had these privileges.

SALLY JO

TINY

Even MU-MUU

Of course, she was told it was "out of the question."

Why, oh why did she have such an unreasonable owner?

It wasn't as if she were asking to go running around Central Park at night

At the very least, she deserved a new collar.

R. Chast

Welcome to... CAMP MANDATORY FUN!

Here's where you'll have lots of fun... or else!

Ha, ha. Only kidding. But let's play some volleyball! C'mon!!

Oh, boy! What a great game. Time to toast up some marshmallows!

You'll meet lots of people your very own age here, by the way.

Oops! Time for our daily swim in the lake! It's so refreshing! Everyone has to go!

Yay! It's lunchtime!

Guess what? Now we get to make some arts and crafts!

The fun never stops!

See you soon!

The Talking Duck

Once there was this guy who taught his duck to talk.

It was really amazing. The duck had a working vocabulary of about 43 words.

me · hi · duck · food · Mama · want · Dada · boy · girl

Today's Duck magazine even ran its feature story on him.

Today's Duck
THE TALKING DUCK— MIRACLE OR MADNESS? SEE PAGE 3

The trouble was, in spite of everything, this duck was really not all that bright.

X RAY INTO HEAD

In fact, he was actually quite a pain.

He kept repeating his words and phrases over and over again.

Me want cereal · Duck. · Where ball? · Mama. · Me duck

It began to drive the poor guy bats.

Duck duck me duck you duck duck DUCK, DUCK DUCKDUCK!!!

The guy tried to get him to shut up, but it was too late. He was a talker and there was no going back.

How about some of your favorite cereal? · Duck duc duck duc duck d duc d

One day, he reached the end of his rope and dropped the duck off at the House of Hotcakes.

HOUSE OF HOTCAKES

R. Chast

 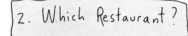

ORDERING CHINESE

1. The Decision

"Let's order Chinese!"

"Fine with me!"

2. Which Restaurant?

Szechuan Delite — TAKE OUT MENU

Szechuan Chimes — TAKE OUT 201-69??

BIG WOK — FREE DELIVERY

SZECHUAN ATTIC

3. Things One Almost Always Orders

Cold Sesame Noodles

Apricot Chicken

  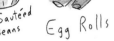

Dried Sautéed String Beans

Egg Rolls

Moo Shu Pork

4. Things One Never Orders

Braised Calf Brain in Happy Sauce

Milk Curd in Two Parts

Sweet-and-Sour Ox

5. The Wait

6. Arrival

Szechuan Chimes

7. The Extras

Orange

Four Fortune Cookies

Packets of Soy Sauce, Duck Sauce, & Mustard

White Rice

THE STORE OF DOOM

In our neighborhood, there is a store that seems to have a lot of problems.

To be more precise, it is really the locale that has the problems, since it has been at least six different stores in the last eight years.

It is surrounded by bakeries, banks, shoe stores, delis, boutiques, and many other places that seem to thrive.

So what is the matter with this place?

Is there some ancient merchant's curse on the building?

In its recent past, it has been: home to an architectural firm—

KEEBLE, FISK & LOWE ARCHITECHTS

a bath accessories shop—

TOWEL 'n' TILE

a health-food restaurant—

Garden of Eden

a lamp emporium—

THE LIGHT HOUSE

a child's clothing boutique –

and lastly, a cut-rate electronics store which folded about three months ago.

At this very moment, workmen are blocking up the _entire_ _back_ of the store with cinderblocks.

Who knows why?

Maybe this will turn their fortunes around.

But it is doubtful.

The new owners may see their place as "Helen and Hank's Camera Cupboard" –

but everyone else will see only THE STORE OF DOOM.

THE END

R. Chast

AUGUST 1988

CULTURAL EVENTS CALENDAR FOR THE TOSSLE LAKE COMMUNITY

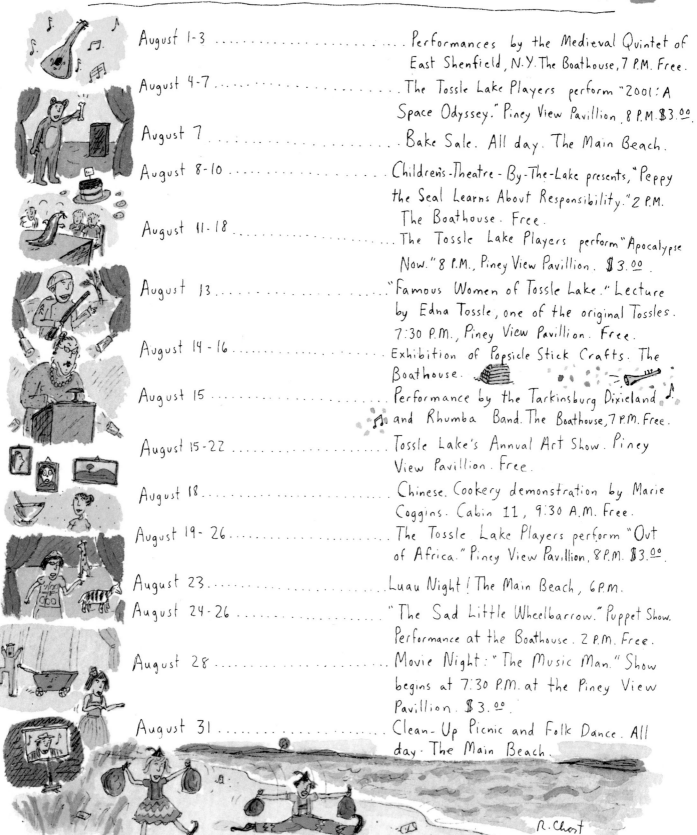

August 1-3 .... Performances by the Medieval Quintet of East Shenfield, N.Y. The Boathouse, 7 P.M. Free.

August 4-7 .... The Tossle Lake Players perform "2001: A Space Odyssey." Piney View Pavillion, 8 P.M. $3.00.

August 7 .... Bake Sale. All day. The Main Beach.

August 8-10 .... Children's-Theatre-By-The-Lake presents, "Peppy the Seal Learns About Responsibility." 2 P.M. The Boathouse. Free.

August 11-18 .... The Tossle Lake Players perform "Apocalypse Now." 8 P.M., Piney View Pavillion. $3.00.

August 13 .... "Famous Women of Tossle Lake." Lecture by Edna Tossle, one of the original Tossles. 7:30 P.M., Piney View Pavillion. Free.

August 14-16 .... Exhibition of Popsicle Stick Crafts. The Boathouse.

August 15 .... Performance by the Tarkinsburg Dixieland and Rhumba Band. The Boathouse, 7 P.M. Free.

August 15-22 .... Tossle Lake's Annual Art Show. Piney View Pavillion. Free.

August 18 .... Chinese Cookery demonstration by Marie Coggins. Cabin 11, 9:30 A.M. Free.

August 19-26 .... The Tossle Lake Players perform "Out of Africa." Piney View Pavillion, 8 P.M. $3.00.

August 23 .... Luau Night! The Main Beach, 6 P.M.

August 24-26 .... "The Sad Little Wheelbarrow." Puppet Show. Performance at the Boathouse. 2 P.M. Free.

August 28 .... Movie Night: "The Music Man." Show begins at 7:30 P.M. at the Piney View Pavillion. $3.00.

August 31 .... Clean-Up Picnic and Folk Dance. All day. The Main Beach.

R. Chast

AT SHOE LEVEL

Last week, we were all sitting around, like we always do, right under the big tree in the Ames' front yard.

There was Hank, Dodie, Nancy, Ben, and me.

We were all talking about — I don't know — gravel or something, when Ben said he thought he'd go lie down for a while.

Well, we weren't too terribly alarmed or anything. Maybe it was that pumpernickel crumb he'd eaten for lunch.

He kind of slunk off behind a root. Anyway, we kept talking and talking ~

— until suddenly, what should appear from where Ben was "lying down", but one of those HUGE DISGUSTING FLYING THINGS !!!!!!

We could hardly believe it. All of us had made promises to one another about how we weren't going to turn into one of those.

YUCK.

They were so show-offy and made no sense.

I'm a flower!

NOTE SIZE OF HEAD

Just as we expected, Ben almost immediately started treating us differently.

How's the air DOWN THERE?

And by the next day, he had all these awful new friends.

You know, there are times when it wouldn't bother me at all if he wound up in an old mayonnaise jar with holes punched in the lid.

But then I think, poor Ben — maybe he couldn't help it.

R. Chast

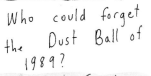
THE OLDEN DAYS

Who could forget the Dust Ball of 1989?

One had to come in costume.

Some people were so imaginative, like the Meechams.

Bodley Newworth had a card or two up his sleeve, as well.

Remember Ninny Tent and the cousin she dragged along?

He just wasn't used to our shenanigans.

Of course, the Redgers were there, as dull as nails.

You couldn't pry fun out of them with a crowbar.

Why they always came to these parties, we'll never know.

A PARAKEET'S FIRST LOOK
at the
UNIVERSE

Hello, budgie!

Do you like your cage? Good.

But now, we're going to explore the world outside! Let's start with the kitchen. Come on! C'mon out!! Here, pretty!!!

Test your wings... that's right!

Shall we try the livingroom?

But what's this? It's an open window!

Nice going, little bird! Here's some interesting stuff-buildings, trees, etc.

Now we're so-o-o high... it's Cloud World!

There's a lot of different types, but you won't be tested on it

We're going up a lot higher now.

Here's where we leave Earth and head out into Space.

Say goodbye to the Solar System, budgie!

Who knows where you're headed.

It's vaster than you imagined... and some things "out there" look a little weird.

But at least that beats those big areas of nothing. Talk about depressing!!!

Well, that's about enough for today. Time to head back!

Here you go.

See you next week!

R. Chast

La Bohème

PRINCIPAL PLAYERS

Marcello - (In advertising)

Rodolpho - (Very junior partner in law firm)

Colline - (Pre-med)

Schaunard - (Computer programmer)

Mimi - (sec'y at Happywear, Inc.)

These five chums all live in the same crummy, six-story walk-up near 1st Ave. in N.Y.C.

The four fellows share a one-bedroom on the top floor.

QUADRUPLE LOFT BEDS

Mimi lives on the floor beneath them in a tiny studio.

Rodolpho and Mimi meet at a "tenant's meeting" and really hit it off.

I don't like tofu.

Nor do I.

Mimi suddenly breaks off singing and has a coughing fit.

KOFF KOFF KOFF KOFF KOFF

In a beautiful aria, Mimi sings of how the landlord either doesn't send up any heat, or he sends up so much it messes up her sinuses.

The others chime in, about that same problem, plus many others.

In a reckless burst of enthusiasm, Rodolpho sings of how he is going to sue their landlord.

The very next day, they all receive notices to vacate their apartments by the following weekend.

Uh-oh.

Marcello, Rodolpho, Colline, and Schaunard manage to find a nice oversized studio on 158th Street and Lenox Ave.

It's only $695.00 a month!

Mimi, on the other hand, moves to an obscure neighborhood on the edge of Queens and is never heard from again.

FIELDCREST PARK?

GOLLYDOT HILLS?

NEW JECKLE MEADOW?

GRIM MARSH?

SLOW GARDENS?

R. Chast

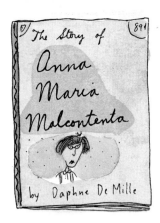

IT'S JUST ONE DAY A YEAR

Marvin was the sort of guy who really went in for medieval festivals.

Fortunately, one came around to the fairgrounds just outside his town every October.

For the entire month before, Marvin flooded the house with medieval music.

Simple, quaint, and eventually grating, these tunes wafted through the den, into the kitchen, and finally, outside.

It was Marvin's way of getting everyone as worked up as possible about the approaching event.

Wait... you're going to *love* this next one.

The day it came to town, he was really very excited.

Marvin, calm down.

Dad, you're getting really hyper.

What's the big deal, Dad?

Even though it was cold and drizzly, he loaded everyone into the car, and off they went.

When they got there, Marvin just walked around, absorbing all the medievalness.

TINKA·TINKA·TINK·TINK·

Not everyone shared his enthusiasm, but that wasn't his problem.

Marvin, the children's feet are wet.

R. Chast

MONDO BOXO

MON-DO BOXO

"MONDO BOXO"
by LTN²
© 1924, 1954, 1993

A BOXLY BOOK
4117 E. 79ᵗʰ Street
NEW YORK, N.Y.

Meet the Box family!

Dad   Mom   Tots

They live here, at 121 Old Box Lane.

The living room.

They have one antique.

It was made in the "Pre-Box" days. (P.B.)

They keep it in a box.

Anyway, here are some typical boxes:

very popular

tiny, hard to manufacture, & expensive

passé

somewhat popular

The Box family is actually very happy. One of their fave hobbies is "stacking."

"Knocking over" is also a ton of fun.

HA-HA

Everyone goes to school.

A GOOD BOX IS A HAPPY BOX

Some go to college and study special topics like~

SQUARE ROOTS $\sqrt{9,397}$

$\sqrt{1/2}$ $\sqrt{7}$

BOXING

CUBISM

It's pretty much of a utopia.

See ya "around" [ha ha]

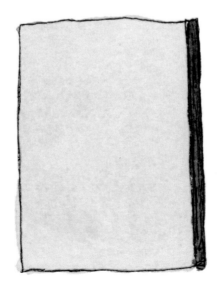

LE TEMPS PERDU

Propriety – large families –
feminine modesty – Life
with Father – big Sunday
dinners

The '20's –

Reckless youth – crazy
parties – abandonment –
gin, gin, and more gin –
Paris by ocean liner

The '30's –

Golden age of cinema –
the rich – Art Deco –
madcap tin heiresses

The '50's –

Wholesomeness – innocence –
high school – milk shakes –
suburbia – not being "weird"

The '60's –

Geometric things –
social change – experimentation –
drugs – unlikely heroes

R. Chast

Letter from Rio

Dearest Fiona,
It had been a summer of almost unbearable loneliness and the eating of Chinese food in bulk.

My mother was sick in Bayonne, New Jersey.

There was a man in my building who was weird and liked to torment me.

You! You're my enemy!!!

I was always afraid that the telephone would ring and I would have to deal with something,

or that it would ring in the middle of the night and wake me up, terrifying me with a sinister wrong number.

R-R-RING!!!

One day at the supermarket, I bought a can of peas.

Little Sweeties
PEAS

When I opened it, I found, to my surprise, it contained a map of Brazil.

BRAZIL

This was so unusual an occurence that I took it as a sign to pack up and GO.

So I left. I took a cab to the airport and bought a ticket to Rio de Janiero.

So long!

It was lovely when I arrived. There was a mambo band, and everyone was dressed in white.

I'm never coming back. Regards to everybody, mom and all.

Love,
Miranda
XXX's & OOO's

R. Chast

SELECTIONS FROM
THE SLICED PEACH
.COLLECTION
OF SHELLEY B.

Happy Sliced Peaches
Briartree, Minnesota
October 15, 1961

Verigood Sliced Peaches
Sheldon, Wisconsin
February 8, 1963

Ambrosia Sliced Peaches
Surplus City, Nebraska
September 20, 1964

Jumpin' Jehosephat
Sliced Peaches
Mildwood, Kentucky
May 12, 1968

Wepackum Sliced
Peaches
Lake Veal, Iowa
March 17, 1970

Honey Sliced Peaches
Huldro Corners, Illinois
November 5, 1971

G'n'L Sliced
Peaches
Byzantium, North Dakota
April 19, 1975

Generic Sliced Peaches
Nicety, Missouri
July 30, 1979

Oh-So-Good Sliced Peaches
Tantamount, New Mexico
June 11, 1982

Halcyon Sliced Peaches
East Pern, Idaho
December 1, 1985

R. Chast

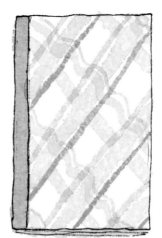

This book is dedicated to

Doris   Boris

Morris & Cloris

ELLEN JAY FLANDERS'

A NEW YORK EVENING

The air was seasonably cold and everyone (almost) was dressed appropriately.

It was not winter in Moscow, but it may as well have been,

except that in the chilly air, Manhattan glittered like a diamond.

Everybody who was anybody was on their way to the castle that night.

The Duchess of Oats would surely be there.

← Tiara (worth an arm and a leg!)

As well as Count Clothesly.

Hopefully, the Baron and Baroness Von Hodgepodge would arrive!

Others invited were the Duke of Strange

and the Marquis of the Van Allen Belt.

A little servant wearing some lovely togs came around bearing refreshments.

Then everyone took their seats in the main dining hall.

First course was a wonderful, clear broth of truffles—

served with a delightful bread.

An interesting pasta was then brought to the table by a host of tiny beings,

followed by a salad that was grown on the castle grounds.

Everyone partook of the delightful cookies.

Men and women alike retired to the library for brandy and a smoke.

The conversation drifted from Angola to circular farming,

to how much everyone despised goldfish

to Venice in the Fall, after the tourists left.

All too soon, everyone rang for their chauffeurs.

GOOD NIGHT, EVERYBODY!

Fred

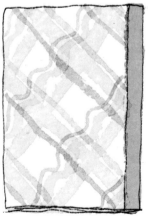

BUS INCIDENT #1

R. Chast

A PUBLIC SERVICE ANNOUNCEMENT FROM THE
POSTURE POLICE

Stand up straight or we'll haul you in!

Look at this one— curled up like a little anchovy.

Our radar picks stuff like that right up!

You're UNDER ARREST.

Offenders then have to spend at least 24 hours in the Slumpers' Cell.

After that, we make 'em watch a couple of educational films.

BAD POSTURE: HIGHWAY TO HELL

Hope we don't see you around!

R. Chast

The World of Choice

Now that all the chores were done, what should he do next?

He could write a letter to Klenso® Soap, telling somebody over there how much he liked their product.

Maybe they'd even send him a case of Klenso®!

But somehow, that seemed kind of sleazy.

Take a gander at all the free soap I got!

He could invite Nat over, but there was always a chance that Nat could make an off-hand remark that would cause him either to worry or would hurt his feelings.

How come you're wearing such a weird shirt?

He could take a Nature Walk, but he wasn't really that sort of guy.

SIGH

It crossed his mind to stroll up and down Creosote Avenue where all the shops were,

but it was a pretty safe bet that he'd come home with a book he would never read, some odd trinket, or a bar of scented soap he didn't need.

Perhaps he'd just sit for a little while longer. After all, was there a law against it?

r. Chast

A LITTLE EXCURSION

It was just another Friday night in Teppersburg.

We could stay home and watch TV, do chores, read, etc.,

— or we could take a drive out to Martinsville, about 18 miles down County Road.

The trip won out, especially when we saw in the local paper who was playing at Buffoon's.

Hey, honey — guess what?!

It was none other than the Chihuahua Sisters.

No!!

Our neighbor's daughter, Pam, agreed to sit for the kids.

I wore a dress that was nice, but not too showy.

Pants would have been just fine, too.

The place wasn't but half full.

Who noticed though, when the Sisters sang their #1 hit, "Two Leaf Clover"?

I had about 1¾ of a gin-and-tonic, but my husband had 3, so I drove home.

The kids woke up as soon as we pulled into the driveway.

R. Chast

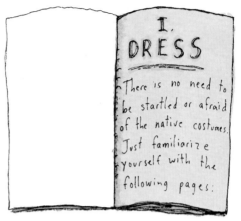

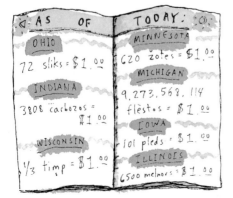

The Wandering Mathematician

He's good at all kinds of math - addition, subtraction, multiplication - even division!

Having trouble with your checkbook, budget, homework, etc.? Just give him a call.

He'll be over in two shakes of a little lamb's tail!

Even if it's not an emergency, he's happy to make the trip.

I was just wondering... what's a SINE?

So don't settle for one of those cut-rate imitators.

The Roving Calculator

The Travelling Reckoner

Zendor, The Migratory Arithmetician

Get the real thing.

R. Chast

The Trail Elves

Some people had all the luck and wound up in the Girl Scouts.

Others, for one reason or another, joined off-brand groups like the Fireplace Girls.

But no brand was more off-brand than the notorious Trail Elves.

Other girls came to school wearing blue or khaki or whatever outfits the day their groups had meetings.

Trail Elves had to wear empty appliance boxes.

Other organizations had badges like Arts & Crafts, First Aid, etc.

Trail Elves had Watching TV and Setting Clocks.

The big deal was that instead of the 10¢ dues that everybody else paid, Trail Elves' dues were only 7¢.

Despite what many parents believed, it just wasn't worth the three-cent savings.

R. Chast

DAISY STEPS OUT

I'll never forget that day: May 18, 1973.

But first, let me backtrack a little. I'm just your average dairy cow.

I'd lived all my life on a medium-sized farm in Lincoln, Vermont.

I had nice parents, nice friends.

"Moo" "DADS" "mom" "SPOTTY"

Even the man who owned the farm was kind of a decent guy.

Chow time!

Everything was just dandy, but it was dull: D-U-L-L.

The day I saw the pick-up truck go by on route 83, I figured it was now or never.

Just one long running jump, and I'd be in like Flynn.

It's hard to believe, but I made it. The truck was holding a couple of cows and a sheep.

It just so happened that they were being driven to a dairy farm in New Jersey.

However, I was headed for New York.

Within two weeks, I had a vacant lot to call my own.

R. Chast

18 Octobre

My dear Alice,

Where are all those flowers of yesteryear? Where did they go? Did we place them all in the upstairs closet? — Or you know how Mummy loved so to hide things!

Yesterday did not go so well for me. My dear, darling dog, Little Stick, was hit on the head with a cornice. She has expired. All concerned can pay their respects tomorrow at 8 A.M. at Tiny-Chapel-By-the-Mill.

Do you remember Elsie Vespermichel? She has learned Bridge. Not the regular sort, but the Four-Cornered-Hat version which she claims to have absorbed in its entirety from a Duke. Now there's a turnaround for you.

As for my feet, they improve with the passing of each setting sun. Dr. Hargreaves prescribed a medicine that causes my hair to stand on end. Remember him?

Dell Flowrine has had her baby. It is

a boy. How unfortunate that her husband has lost all his money in the Whiting-Grimsby scandal. Do you recall their parlour on Vanning Street? The shutters, the cupboard doors & c., lying this way and that, awaiting hinging? The tiny shell-and-cup pattern around the molding that was all but obscured in the Big Flood? What fun we used to have.

I have no ill-will left toward any of the Mosley-Brooks. You may pass the word along.

_Do_ write, chérie.

Fondly,
Irma

ONE THING AFTER ANOTHER

Sometimes you are looking at something quite harmless—

—when suddenly, a wave of anxiety and nausea overtakes you!

Anxiety OUT OF NOWHERE!!!

You try to trace it back... was it somebody's name?

Perhaps his name just sounded like something you didn't want to think about...

Something to do with BOAT?

Maybe it was just ol' Joe himself making you a little "nervous in the service"!

No? You only knew him to say hello to?

Well, now it's safe to say you really have a problem.

R. Chast

MAIDS from SPACE

No one knew what part of the universe they came from.

All we knew was, one day they weren't here—

GREASY SMUDGE CAT HAIRS DUST BALL

—and the next day, precisely at 9 A.M., there they were, standing in the foyer.

All they said was, "we're from the Agency."

They seemed pretty well-prepared.

O.K., so maybe at first we had a few reservations.

NO!!!

But we relaxed.

CRASH!

They had to leave at 5 o'clock, and no later.

Every Tuesday until the Earth finally went off its axis, it was the same thing.

R. Chast

KAREN'S FOOT'S STORY

Just this afternoon, I had the strangest dream...

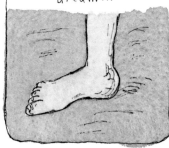

Karen was sitting in a funny position, and after 20 minutes, I felt myself start to doze off.

Blah blah blah

Z-Z-Z-Z-Z

I know this will sound silly, but I dreamed that there was another foot, exactly *like* *me* - only the exact reverse.

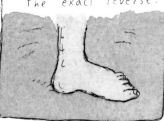

We fell completely in love.

He was a totally different type of foot from that jerk next door.

We were both wearing the most beautiful, elegant socks I'd ever seen.

All of a sudden, I could feel us run side by side, laughing, through a grassy meadow.

Right about then, good old Karen must have moved her leg, because I started to wake up...

HUH?? WHA??

Back to reality. Oh, well!

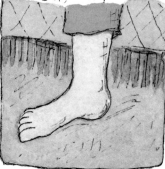

R. Chast

THE OLDEN DAYS II

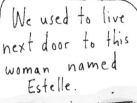

We used to live next door to this woman named Estelle.

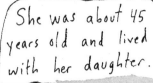

She was about 45 years old and lived with her daughter.

She was a waitress in a lounge.

Who knew where, except it was in Brooklyn someplace.

Sometimes when I was sick and home from school, she'd "sit" for me.

One time she brought over one of the outfits she wore at work.

She read movie magazines aloud.

Bobby Darin in fight at El Morocco!

I liked her lots.

My mother disliked her because she made up "wild stories."

So me and my boyfriend decide to take a helicopter to St. Thomas, and the helicopter gets stuck and we wind up in a...

R. Chast

A True Story

Dear Discover:

I started coinshooting one year ago and I'm hooked on it. I first got started when I read stories in treasure magazines. I got interested in buying a metal detector and bought a White's 2/DB Series 2 and in a few months I found enough coins to pay for the detector.

But I couldn't stop there.

Once I had that detector in my hands, I couldn't let it go.

After it paid for itself, it soon started paying for everything else.

MEALS

CLOTHING

← RENT

Eventually, my boss called me into his office and said, "Looky here, if you like metal detecting so much, why don't you go into it full-time, if you catch my drift?"

In short, I was fired.

ACME CORPORATION

Luckily, I had no family, or it would have been a much bigger deal.

Months went by.

MAY
APRIL
MARCH

Then, one fateful day, I met a girl who had a thing about clouds.

I could swear that's a cumulonimbus.

She and I continue to see quite a bit of each other.

No, maybe it's a nimbostratus.

Unless I find something "interesting," we are usually pretty poor.

Honey? I think this is a 1924 series GH penny!!!

Even so, you couldn't find a happier pair.

Thanks again— Best wishes, Harry Brant

r. Chast

A Guide To Yard Sales

Do not buy old tin cans, even if they are only 10¢.

Be a little bit careful with what you find amusing.

It is perfectly okay, however, to chuckle at ridiculously overpriced items.

Generally speaking, pets, children, houses themselves, and what the person is wearing are not for sale.

If the baked goods look even halfway tasty, be a sport and sample a couple.

Remember to say "thank you," even if you are burning up with embarrassment from not buying anything.

R. Chast

MABEL "overly creative" VERNE

Here she is!

You took a chance if you gave her a set of dishtowels.

Next time you visited, they might be reincarnated as curtains—

Oh, they're LOVELY.

Or appear as tiny "throw" rugs.

Oh, my.

Conversely, if she needed dishtowels, chances are she wouldn't go out and buy some.

No, she'd whip them up out of an old pair of pants.

R. Chast

Science Corner

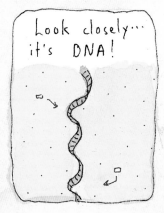

R. Chast

The Mysterious Opera

That afternoon, we were listening to the radio.

They were playing an opera in a language we did not recognize. It may have been Norwegian.

We were trying to figure out what was going on, trying to decipher a word here and there—

KREML
EINSKA
HEYILSKA
LEFSA
INSKA

or picking up a clue from the music.

There were no intermissions. There seemed to be a cast of millions.

One scene had background music that sounded like a washing machine.

Soon after that, a tenor intoned a word that sounded like "PICABI-TUT" over and over again.

PICABI-TUT
PICABI-TUT
PICABI-T
PICABI
PIG

Out of nowhere, cymbals would start clanging for 30 seconds.

CLANG
CLANG

Then there was a soprano that made Jim think of Rapunzel.

Another scene reminded Ellen of the terrible flying monkeys of The Wizard of Oz.

Mostly it was very boring, but it was so odd we couldn't shut it off.

What could it be? It was definitely modern.

R. Chast

The MAGIC MOUNTAIN

AS TOLD WITH PENS

One day, a pen went to visit another pen in a pen sanitarium.

Heard you're not feeling up to snuff!

At first he hated it, but then it started to grow on him.

I can see how this has its charms.

He met a lot of other interesting writing implements.

"Dime"

"Bleh"   "Moderno"   "Fontano"   "Clicky"

He kept wishing that he was ill like the pen he was visiting, so he could finish some of the conversations he'd started, especially the ones with Clicky.

I hate typewriters.

Me, too.

Joy of joys! He turned out to be a little under par himself.

It's just a little spot on the barrel.

He wound up staying seven years.

So, uh, what do YOU think about typewriters?

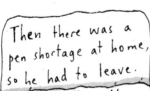

Then there was a pen shortage at home, so he had to leave.

Where's the goddamn pen... I just had it a minute ago..

HERE you are.

NEXT WEEK:

THE ALL-PEN VERSION OF "GONE WITH THE WIND"

r. Chast

THE FLAN MAN

Other neighborhoods had their Mister Freezee's, their Dairy Swirlos...

We had the Flan Man.

Even from ten blocks away, you could hear his little song:

Yo-de-do-do, Who's got the FLAN! You cook it on the stove In a little white PAN·

Wait, there's more.

You have to let it cool, So the stuff can GEL. Then you'll get the flan That you LOVE SO WELL.

We'd all try to hide, but for some reason certain people thought it was terrific stuff and would make us go out and get some.

Hurry! You're going to miss the Flan Man !!!

There was only the one flavor, but there were three sizes to choose from.

TOO MUCH

MUCH TOO MUCH

HORSE-CHOKER

For a short while, he sold Flan Shakes, but they really bombed.

Try our shakes, They're really tasty You won't find 'em Gross or pasty.

One day, he didn't show up.

YIPPEE!   YAHOO!

CLICK

But just a month later, all the wind got taken out of our sails.

FLAN KING

R. Chast

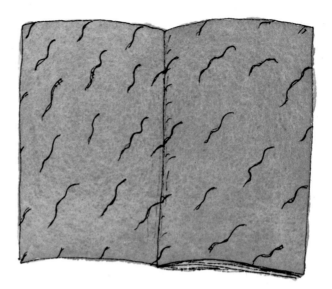

To various birds
I have owned.
~ Anna

Well, it's quite a
piece of thread
we have here.

People have come
from far and wide
to admire it.

Sometimes they
can hardly believe
it, but there
it is.

They even built
a new wing for it
over at the
Museum of Things.

When you leave,
make sure to
get a postcard.

They cost maybe
25¢, so buy a
couple.

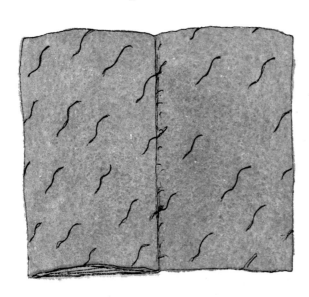

How Are Clichés Made?

Most clichés in the U.S. are manufactured at the Clichéworld plant in Mattawan, New Jersey.

But the process starts long before then, oftentimes at the breakfast table of one of our employees.

Another day, another dollar.

DING

The cliché is then carefully wrapped in plastic and rushed into the Examination Room for testing.

How many times a day can you say it?

Who can say it?

Is it easy to remember?

Is it REAL CATCHY?

If it passes muster, the cliché is sent to the lab to be fully analyzed and encoded.

Only when it has been thoroughly sorted out can production begin...

Another day, another dollar.

Another day, another dollar.

Another day, another dollar.

and before you can say Jack Robinson, it'll be in your life.

Ah well, another day, another dollar.

By the By by Mr. X

Did you know that 2 cups equal 1 pint, 2 pints equal 1 quart, 4 quarts equal one gallon? Sure surprised me!... Bert Niswansky, of route 8, is looking for any stamps with animals on them... Saw Mrs. and Ms. Jiblette in the Food Basket out on route 92 the other day. Mrs. Jiblette was buying ground chuck, a container of half-and-half, and some "living gloves"! What does it all mean?... The leaves are turning again... Why did the guy throw the clock out the window? Ask Bill Hedgison... Spotted Esti and Mark Posner at the Mart-o-Food on County Drive a few days ago. Esti knocked over a display of triangular-shaped cheeses. Was her face red!... The atomic weight of Yttrium is 88.905... The Finderley boy, Mike, isn't doing too well in math. Any suggestions?... Remember Grandma's spice cake? It sure was tasty... Who's rooting for Freemont High's Flyers? I know I am... A word to the wise: a stitch in time saves nine... New restaurant at the Jumbo Mall: Sage. I hear they make a mean burger and that their ambulance is very pleasant... How did you like all that rain last week? Yours truly got _soaked_!... Well, "see" you soon. Toodle-loo!

R. Chost

POSTCARD FOLDER FROM SUBURBIA

FAMILY CIRCLE

The Marvinsons weren't sure whether to be sad or proud when their son was tested in school and found to be a crank.

All the instructor had done was ask "what's your favorite sandwich, little Fred?"

And all Fred had done was reply, "None of your business, you gigantic ass."

From then on, Fred was placed in the class for the exceptionally cranky.

This was a completely different class from the really dangerous kids.

I'm gonna CUT YO FACE.

These were just the chronic nitpickers, whiners, and complainers whom the teachers and other students couldn't stand to have in their classes.

Get him OUT OF HERE!!!

The simplest lesson turned into a big problem.

I hate this topic, and I hate YOU. May I be excused?

It was incredible that the Marvinsons could feel even the tiniest bit of pride in their pain-in-the-neck offspring, but they did.

Yes, he just gets crankier and crankier every day!

After all, he was their flesh and blood.

R. Chast

HIGHLIGHTS
OF THE
PAUL BUNYAN TOUR
1989

① Our first stop was Evansview, Idaho, to see Lucille Van Troast's collection of Paul Bunyan's socks – very inspiring.

② After that, we made a brief sojourn to Needley, Idaho, to take in the Museum of Babe

③ Then came the LONG HAUL – down to Lake Salvo, Florida to visit the offices of Bunyaniana, our crowd's favorite magazine!

④ And finally, we all made it to the home of a woman in Maine who claimed to have found a hat belonging to P.B. "while weeding her garden." We left unconvinced of its authenticity.

R. Chast

OUR FRIEND RUTH

My sister and I used to live in a small house in Canarsie, along with our folks.

O.K., so it wasn't much, but we owned it.

We had this friend Ruth who came over a lot.

We lived the life of Reilly. If we got bored, we'd go visit Ruth's mom, who was a hairdresser at Mr. Antonio's.

The best was when one of her "regulars" was there, and we'd watch her do the same style on the same lady for the 50th time.

We'd just laugh our heads off.

Mr. Antonio would get really furious, so we'd act scared and run out screaming.

Then Ruth would take us to a luncheonette that gave out free water.

I wonder what became of her.

 # A VISIT FROM STAN

When cousin Stan came into town, we always got out of our doldrums.

SIGH   SIGH   SIGH

There was no one in the world we'd like less to bore.

So, you <u>see</u>, I've really been keeping up with my stamp collecting.

Can we change the subject?

Usually Connie, Margery, and I ate at home, and if we went out at all, is was to a comfortable, neighborhoody place like the Tabletop.

THE TABLE TOP

It wasn't any great shakes, but you knew what to expect.

How's your filet of sole, Connie? HA, HA, HA, HA

Anyway, Stan said he was coming into town on Tuesday night, so we made a reservation at a place we'd only vaguely heard about.

It was called 23479, and it was located almost as far downtown as you could go, on a tiny street called Collie Lane.

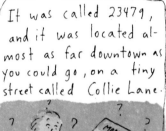

MANHATTAN

No one had ever heard of this street.

Finally, it was Tuesday night. Stan arrived. Even though we all liked him, he made us kind of nervous.

After a few minutes of chit-chat, we all got into a taxi and told our driver where our destination lay.

The first part of the ride was quite familiar, but after 5 minutes, we were in a part of town none of us had ever seen before.

We passed streets with outlandish names. Had we fallen asleep and been hijacked to Teaneck?

STATE STREET
PERRY BOULEVARD

Strangely enough, when we looked out the back window, we could see the tops of the Chrysler and Empire State buildings.

There were no people on the street.

We went by a restaurant that did not seem completely unfamiliar to me, although I could not tell why.

Escanaba

As far as we knew, we had not passed over any bridges or through any tunnels.

We were completely baffled and disoriented, but who wanted to let Stan know?

This is great!

The taxi turned onto a side street that had a row of yellowish white brick houses on either side. I remember that it was very steep...

... and finally, we were on Collie Lane. The fare came to $3.10, which struck us as oddly low, but we weren't about to make a fuss.

Here ya are!

23479 wasn't hard to find.

It was just about the strangest-looking restaurant I'd even been in.

The entire place was about 9 feet wide, 30 feet deep, and about 40 feet high from floor to ceiling.

It was very dimly lit. The walls were greyish blackish green. There were 3 booths, 2 of which were full.

It was scary but exciting.

The other patrons seemed nonplussed, so we tried to follow suit. Stan looked like he was having a pretty good time.

The food was pretty good, but difficult to remember.

The ride back to our apartment seemed much quicker. We dropped Stan off at his hotel on the way.

BYE!!!

A couple of weeks later, we tried to go there again, but we couldn't find it.

Collie Lane? Never heard of it, pal.

r. Chast